Redbeard's Kingdom

Anthony Holcroft

Redbeard's Kingdom

Illustrated by Timothy Ide

Omnibus
DIPPER

Scholastic Publications Ltd,
Villiers House,
Clarendon Avenue,
Leamington Spa,
Warks CV32 6EB, UK

Scholastic Inc.,
730 Broadway, New York, NY 10003, USA

Ashton Scholastic Pty Ltd,
PO Box 579, Gosford, New South Wales,
Australia

Ashton Scholastic Ltd,
Private Bag 1, Penrose, Auckland,
New Zealand

First published by Omnibus Books, part of the Ashton Scholastic Group, 1991
This edition, only available as part of Scholastic Literacy Centre: Fiction
(Green Set), first published in the UK by Scholastic Publications Ltd, 1995

ISBN 0 590 53536 6

Omnibus Dipper is a registered trademark of Ashton Scholastic Pty Ltd

Printed and bound in Great Britain by
Cox & Wyman Ltd, Reading, Berkshire

10 9 8 7 6 5 4 3 2 1

Redbeard's Kingdom

Redbeard's Castle

The Royal Wheatfields

The Royal Orchards

Ford

Wisewoman's Hut

The Royal Wheatfields

Boundary Fence

Blackbeard's Castle

The Royal Orchards

Blackbeard's Kingdom

Redbeard

Blackbeard

There was once an island ruled by two
brothers. Their names were Redbeard
and Blackbeard, and their kingdoms each
covered one-half of the island. In each there
was a wheatfield, an orchard and a wood.
A sparkling river ran through the wheatfields, bees hummed among the flowers in
the orchards, and birds sang in the woods.
There was always plenty to eat, and everyone was happy.

One day Redbeard went out to look at his field. The wheat was almost ripe, and a forest of golden stems rippled in the breeze.

The king gazed at his field with pride. "I am the happiest of men," he said. "I have everything I need in this world." But then a niggling little thought crept into his head. "How much nicer it would be," he said to himself, "if there were no boundary between my field and Blackbeard's, for then my wheatfield would stretch to the horizon, and that would be a marvellous sight."

8

Next morning, when Redbeard went to look at his field, he felt even more irritated by the boundary fence; and on the third day he could bear it no longer. "It spoils my view!" he shouted. And he gave orders for the fence to be pulled down and dumped in a big hole.

When Blackbeard heard that his fence
had been destroyed, he was very angry
indeed. He sent a messenger to Redbeard
with a stern warning. If, within twenty-
four hours, a new fence was not standing
in place of the old, his soldiers would
come and trample Redbeard's wheat into
the ground.

Redbeard didn't bother to send a reply. Instead, he ordered his army to invade Blackbeard's kingdom. His soldiers entered stealthily during the night, and took the kingdom without a battle. Blackbeard was arrested and thrown into a dungeon.

Everything on the island now belonged to Redbeard. He owned two woods, two orchards, a river, and a great wheatfield stretching to the far blue edge of the sea.

"Now indeed," said Redbeard, "I am a happy man."

One morning Redbeard woke early and looked out the window. The sun was shining, the wheat was golden, and a light breeze ruffled the woods. "I shall take a stroll," said Redbeard, "and breathe the air of my kingdom." He asked for a hamper of food to be packed, and gave instructions that he was not to be disturbed.

As he walked through the fields, enjoying the morning, a starling alighted on a stem of wheat and began greedily nibbling the ripened grain. Redbeard clapped his hands angrily. "How dare you eat my grain!" he said to the starling. "I forbid you to enter my kingdom."

But the starling merely hopped on to a stem a little further away and called back, "This wheat is as much mine as yours, Redbeard." And he went on pecking away for all he was worth.

"I'll have that bird shot," muttered the king as he stalked on his way.

Soon it began to grow very hot. The royal orchard was nearby, and Redbeard lay down in the shade of an old apple tree to rest. He was beginning to feel drowsy. "In a little while," he murmured with a yawn, "I shall have my lunch." Then he stretched out on the grass and went to sleep.

While he was asleep he dreamed that he was having a tug-of-war over the hamper. A great black monster with sharp claws was tugging at it with its teeth. The king pulled with all his strength, but the creature was too strong, and with a sharp rending noise the hamper suddenly split in two.

Redbeard woke with a start to see a skinny black-and-white cat running off into the bushes with the last of his favourite ham-and-egg sandwiches.

The king stamped his foot. "When I get back," he shouted, "I will have every cat in this kingdom flayed alive."

In the meantime he was very hungry, and his hamper was empty. Then he looked up and saw apples gleaming like small red suns among the leaves of the old apple tree. He reached into the leaves and lazily plucked the reddest and ripest apple he could see. He didn't notice a gaping hole on the underside of the apple, nor did he see the bee hidden inside, sipping the sweet juice. As his hand closed over the apple, the bee stung him sharply on his royal finger.

The king dropped the apple with a shout.

"How dare you!" he screamed. "How *dare* you!"

But the bee was not afraid of Redbeard. "You should learn to keep your fingers out of other people's pies," it said angrily, and flew away.

The king stormed home, nursing his swollen finger. "I will have every bee in this kingdom put to death!" he shouted to the woods and the river and the nodding ears of wheat. "I will have every bird shot, and every cat flayed alive. Let every creature that has breath take heed that *I* am master of this kingdom."

As soon as he got back to the palace,
Redbeard had his horse saddled and set off
to see the wisest woman in the kingdom.

The wise woman lived on the edge of the forest in a humble thatched house. There were no coverings on the floor, and no furniture, and this meant that the king, who was too proud to sit on the floor, had always to stand during his visits. And since the wise woman usually took some time to gather her thoughts, he often had to stand for a very long time indeed.

The king wasted no words. "Today," he snapped, "I caught a bird, a cat and a bee stealing in my kingdom. Moreover, the bird was insolent, the cat ran away, and the bee stung my finger. If this sort of thing is allowed to go on, who knows where it will end? Therefore, I have made up my mind to punish every bird, cat and bee in my kingdom, so that no one shall be in doubt who is master of this island. Tell me how this may best be done."

The wise woman thought for a long time. She said nothing for a whole hour. At last she spoke. "Are you sure you want to do this thing?" she said.

"Of course I'm sure," snapped the king. "I wouldn't be asking you if I wasn't."

"Very well," said the wise woman. "I will tell you what to do. You must build three barns, as large as you can make them, without roofs. Each must be filled to over-flowing with food that is delectable to the birds, cats and bees of this island. Then you must send invitations to His Feathered Majesty, the king of the birds, and to Her Mightiness, the queen of the cats, and to Her Murmurous Majesty, the queen of the bees, inviting them and all their subjects to a grand banquet. When they are all assembled within the barns, take this black chalk and draw three circles, one around each barn. When that is done, you should have no further trouble."

Redbeard grunted his thanks and hurried back to the palace with the stick of black chalk. He lost no time in having three roofless barns built, the tallest in the land, and large enough to house the island's entire population of birds, cats and bees.

People came from far and near to stare and marvel.

"They are to be storehouses for the king's treasure," said one.

"They are granaries," said another, "to house all the wheat in the world."

And then Redbeard's servants came and crammed food into the barns until the sides bulged. In the first barn they put every kind of slug and snail and worm that a bird could possibly wish for. They also put in stacks of fruit: peaches, plums, apples and pears, and, on top, a garland of berries and juicy rosehips.

In the second barn they placed food carefully chosen to be attractive to cats but not offensive to birds: great saucers of cream, and fresh meat, raw and roasted, sprinkled with flowering catmint.

The third barn was filled with the sweetest nectar-bearing flowers.

The people were amazed. "The king is mad," they whispered to each other. "He has gone out of his mind."

Then, on the horizon, there appeared a cloud that grew and grew until it filled half the sky. With it came a great wind of beating wings. Soon the townsfolk saw with amazement that the cloud was really a huge flock of birds, led by a graceful white heron whose wings gleamed in the sun. Suddenly the heron dived straight down into the first barn, and all the birds in a rush after him. From inside could be heard a fluttering and flapping and squawking as they set to and gobbled up all the good things that had been prepared for them.

Scarcely were the birds in the barn than the earth shook with the thunder of padding feet, and on the horizon appeared an army of cats. At their head loped an enormous black cat whose silver whiskers shimmered in the sun. Straight to the middle barn she ran, and all the cats after her. Once inside, they ran everywhere, devouring the stacks of delicious food.

Hardly were the cats in the barn than another great cloud appeared, and with it a humming sound that made the air throb. This time it was a swarm of bees of every size and shape, led by a queen bee whose wings glittered in the sun. When the townspeople saw the bees coming, they fled in all directions, covering their heads with cloaks and jackets and scarves and anything else they could lay their hands on. But as soon as the bees reached the barn filled with flowers, they dived down inside it and began greedily devouring the nectar.

No sooner were all three barns full than the king quickly made a circle around each with the black chalk. Suddenly all the humming and fluttering and purring stopped, and a deadly hush settled. Nothing stirred.

Very cautiously the king peered inside the barns and saw to his astonishment that every living thing had been turned to stone.

Redbeard was delighted. Now there were no birds to eat his grain, no cats to steal his lunch, and no bees to sting his fingers. It was true that he missed being wakened in the mornings by the birds singing outside his bedroom window, and the humming of bees in the sun. "But one can't have everything," he sighed. "And I'm *still* the happiest man alive."

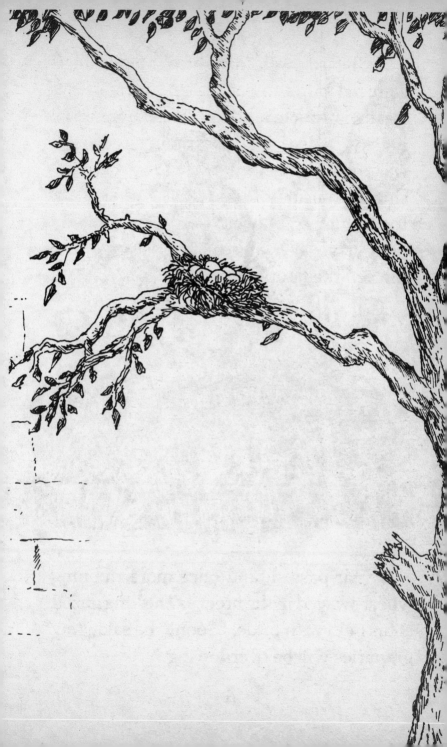

A year passed, and once more ripening wheat swayed in the breeze. The king gazed at his field with pride. "Soon," he said, "my granaries will be overflowing."

But then a terrible thing happened. No sooner was the wheat in ear than a great horde of insects descended on the kingdom. There were so many that they blotted out the sun, and darkness covered the land. They swarmed on to the wheatfield and stripped every stalk of its grain. As far as the eye could see, the wheat was moving with insects. And then, as suddenly, they disappeared. The sun shone again out of a blue sky. But where the swelling harvest had stood, there was now not a grain of wheat to be seen.

The people of the island were in despair. Without the wheat they could make no bread, and without bread there would be famine in the land. And if that wasn't bad enough, there was no fruit in the orchards, and the grass swarmed with mice. Never had anyone seen so many mice. They over-ran the barns and granaries, and even invaded the royal cupboards, tearing holes in the king's velvet robes and nibbling the sleeves of his nightgown as he lay asleep in bed.

Redbeard fled in alarm to the wisest woman in the kingdom. He went down on his knees before her. "Terrible things have been happening," he moaned. "A plague of insects has devoured my wheat, there is no fruit in the orchards, and there are mice everywhere. If something isn't done, we shall all starve to death."

The wise woman sat in silence, stirring only to brush away a mouse that was nibbling the leather thong of her sandal. At length she said, "It is clear to me that your wheat has been devoured because there are no birds to eat the insects. And if there is no fruit in your orchards, it is because there are no bees to pollinate the flowers. And it is hardly surprising that you are plagued with mice when you have no cats. Therefore, the answer is simple: you must quickly replenish your kingdom with birds, cats and bees."

"But how do you expect me to do that," cried Redbeard, "when I have turned them all to stone?"

The wise woman sighed. "You should have thought of that before," she said. "However, by a piece of astonishingly good fortune, I know a spell that will suit your purpose. So listen carefully . . .

Spell for Depetrified

To free oneself from the spells of Gorgons first take the dew from an op

"On the evening of the full moon, which I believe is tonight, you must gather dew from your orchard, enough to fill three clean quart jars. Sprinkle it in a circle around each of the three barns, and this will break the spell and release the creatures inside. But it must be done before sunrise.

"There is one more thing," she added, as Redbeard was about to hurry away. "Everything in the world has its appointed place in the scheme of things. Perhaps you would do well to give some thought to yours."

"I will! I will!" promised the king as he ran out the door.

That night, when the moon rose, everyone in the royal household, including the king himself, rushed out into the orchard to gather dew. It took a long time, but by dawn the three jars were full at last. The king ran to the barns, and with a shaking hand he sprinkled a circle of dew around each one.

At once, with a thunderous roar, the
creatures burst and tumbled out of the
barns. In no time at all the birds had made
short work of the insects, the cats had
pounced on all the mice, and the bees were
busy again in the flowers.

Redbeard inspected the royal granaries and ordered what was left of the grain to be divided equally among his subjects, rich and poor. He released his brother Blackbeard from prison, and gave him both kingdoms to rule. And when he had done that, he retired to live in a small cottage between the orchard and the wheatfield.

He ate his fill from the fruit in the orchard, and slept in the shade of the apple trees, and walked for as long as he liked in the wheatfield with the black-and-white cat at his side.

"It's true," said Redbeard, gazing with love at the orchard and the wheatfield and the distant woods. "I am the happiest man alive."

And this time he really was, for ever after.